# HEiDi HECKELBECK

## Makes a Wish

By Wanda Coven

Illustrated by Priscilla Burris

LITTLE SIMON
New York London Toronto Sydney New Delhi

This book is a work of fiction. Any references to historical events, real people, or real places are used fictitiously. Other names, characters, places, and events are products of the author's imagination, and any resemblance to actual events or places or persons, living or dead, is entirely coincidental.

LITTLE SIMON

An imprint of Simon & Schuster Children's Publishing Division

1230 Avenue of the Americas, New York, New York 10020

First Little Simon hardcover edition May 2016

Copyright © 2016 by Simon & Schuster, Inc.

Also available in a Little Simon paperback edition.

All rights reserved, including the right of reproduction in whole or in part in any form. LITTLE SIMON is a registered trademark of Simon & Schuster, Inc., and associated colophon is a trademark of Simon & Schuster, Inc.

For information about special discounts for bulk purchases, please contact Simon & Schuster Special Sales at 1-866-506-1949 or business@simonandschuster.com.

The Simon & Schuster Speakers Bureau can bring authors to your live event. For more information or to book an event contact the Simon & Schuster Speakers Bureau at 1-866-248-3049 or visit our website at www.simonspeakers.com.

Designed by Ciara Gay

Manufactured in the United States of America 0416 FFG

10 9 8 7 6 5 4 3 2 1

Library of Congress Cataloging-in-Publication Data

Names: Coven, Wanda, author. | Burris, Priscilla, illustator.

Title: Heidi Heckelbeck makes a wish / by Wanda Coven ; illustrated by Priscilla Burris.

Description: First Little Simon hardcover/paperback edition. | New York : Little Simon, 2016. | Series. Heidi Heckelbeck ; 17 | Summary: To undo a disastrous spell, second-grader Heidi Heckelbeck must grant three wishes without magic.

Identifiers: LCCN 2015039409| ISBN 9781481466141 (hc) | ISBN 9781481466134 (pbk) | ISBN 9781481466158 (eBook) .

Subjects: | CYAC: Witches—Fiction. | Wishes—Fiction. | Magic—Fiction. | Schools—Fiction.

Classification: LCC PZ7.C83393 Hko 2016 | DDC [Fic]—dc23

LC record available at http://lccn.loc.gov/2015039409

# CONTENTS

# Chapter 1

# A HO-HUM DAY

"Ho hum." Heidi sighed as she doodled a daisy on her science folder.

Heidi was having a ho-hum morning. She had on a ho-hum outfit. All her favorite clothes were in the wash. She had eaten a bowl of ho-hum oatmeal for breakfast. Henry got the last waffle. And now Heidi and her whole class had to sit and wait for their teacher Mrs. Welli. Mrs. Welli had said she would be right back.

Soon the classroom door squeaked open. Principal Pennypacker followed Mrs. Welli to the front of the room.

*Hmm,* thought Heidi. *I wonder what the principal is doing here?*

Mrs. Welli smiled and clasped her hands. "Principal Pennypacker has a special announcement to make," she said. Then she stepped to one side.

The principal patted the tufts of hair on either side of his head and said, "Good morning, class."

"Good morning, Principal Pennypacker," the class chorused.

The principal

rubbed his hands together. "I have exciting news," he said. "Next week the second grade will go on a field trip to the botanical gardens."

The children all began to talk at once.

Mrs. Welli clapped her hands. "One, two, three—eyes on me!" she said.

Then she nodded for the principal to continue.

"You'll take the school bus to the gardens," he explained. "Once there you'll see flowers, you'll see trees shaped like animals, and you'll even get to play hide-and-seek in a life-size hedge maze. At the end of the visit you will have a class lunch picnic in the fairy garden, followed by ice-cream bars."

"Yay!" cheered the class as they bounced up and down in their seats.

And just like that, Heidi's morning had changed from ho-hum to a real humdinger!

# Chapter 2

# WEATHER GiRL

Heidi plopped her hot-lunch tray onto the table. She always got hot lunch when cheese ravioli was on the menu.

"So, what do you think about the field trip?" she asked her friends.

"Three words," said Lucy Lancaster as she untwisted the cap on her water bottle. "FLOWER POWER FUN."

Everyone at the table cheered and started to giggle.

"Do you think there are real fairies in the fairy garden?" asked Natalie.

"I hope so," Heidi said. Then she squished a whole cheesy pillow of ravioli into her mouth.

"What about rides, like a flower-petal merry-go-round?" asked Laurel Lambert. "I *love* rides."

"It's probably just flowers, plants, and trees," said Bruce Bickerson.

"It's not *just* flowers, plants, and trees," said Heidi. "I've heard they have butterflies and waterfalls."

Lucy peeled an orange. "Well, I'm going to wear my favorite outfit," she said. "And maybe I will also bring my ladybug house, because you never know when you might find a good-luck ladybug."

She chomped an orange slice.

"You'd better think again," Bruce said.

"How come?" asked Lucy, her cheeks full.

"I've got bad news. It's supposed to rain that day," Bruce said.

Bruce always kept up on the weather. It came in handy when he had to test one of his fancy science experiments.

Lucy tossed

her orange peels onto her tray. "Oh no! " she said. "If it rains, they may cancel the trip."

Heidi shook her head. "No way, Lucy!" she said. "It's not going to rain on OUR field trip!"

Then, under her breath, Heidi added, *Because I'm going to make sure the forecast is for sunny skies!*

# Chapter 3

# AN EVERYDAY WISH

Heidi gently lifted her *Book of Spells* from her keepsake box, which she kept under her bed. She smiled at her book as if it were an old friend.

"We have some work to do," she said as she opened the book to the Contents page. Heidi found several

weather spells, but they all called for
ingredients that were hard to find,
like fake eyelashes and purple light-
bulbs. Then she found a spell called
Everyday Wishes. She read it over.

# Everyday Wishes

Do you ever need your room picked up in a hurry? Or perhaps you need a birthday gift and have no time to shop? If you're the kind of witch who needs an ordinary, everyday wish to come true— then this is the spell for you!

Ingredients:

1 straw hat

1 honest wish

2 tablespoons of powdered sugar

1 drop of flower dew

3 lemon gumdrops

Shake the ingredients together in the straw hat. Hold your Witches of Westwick medallion in one hand and place the other over the hat. Chant the following spell:

I Wish I May,
I Wish I Might,
Wish This Wish
so Big aND BRight.

State your honest wish.

Remember to be careful what you wish for.

"This is perfect!" Heidi said out loud. "Now I can wish away the rain."

She jumped off her bed and began to hunt for the ingredients. First, she yanked her straw beach hat from the top shelf in her closet. Then she tiptoed downstairs to the pantry. She plucked three lemon gumdrops from the roof of last year's gingerbread house. She also measured the powdered sugar and placed it in a snack bag.

*Now for the flower dew,* Heidi said to herself. She snuck outside and picked a daisy from Mom's garden. The daisy didn't have any dew on it in the afternoon, but that was not going to stop Heidi.

*I will just sprinkle water on this daisy and make my own flower dew,* she thought. Then she stuck the daisy in a vase with water and took all the ingredients to her room.

She rubbed her hands together
excitedly.

"Look out, storm clouds!" she said.
"Because here comes Heidi. And I'm
bringing the sunshine with me!"

# Chapter 4

# THE BiG DAY

Heidi hopped out of bed early on the day of the field trip. She pulled back the curtain and peeked outside. It was still too dark to tell what kind of day it would be. She dropped the curtain. *No big deal,* she said to herself, *because today will be sunny no matter what!*

Heidi turned over her straw hat and set it on her desk. She emptied the powdered sugar into the hat, followed by the three lemon gumdrops. She dipped her daisy in water and let a single drop fall into the mix. Then she shook the hat gently. Holding her medallion in one hand, she placed her other hand over the mix.

She chanted the spell and made her wish.

"I wish for sunny skies ALL day," Heidi whispered, so as not to wake anyone up. Then she looked out the window. It had gotten light while she had been working her magic.

"Not a cloud in the sky," Heidi said triumphantly. Then she put on her flower-power T-shirt, blue jean skirt, and striped tights. She also slid her favorite butterfly notebook into her backpack.

"Don't forget your raincoats!" called her mother as Heidi and Henry left for school.

Henry grabbed his raincoat off the hook in the mudroom, but Heidi

sailed right past
hers.

"Don't you know
it's supposed to
RAIN?" Henry said.

"That's not what
I heard!" said Heidi.

"You are going
to be SORRY and
SOAKED!" warned Henry.

"Will not!" Heidi shot back.

The bus dropped Heidi's class off
at a grand stone entry gate. A guide

greeted them and led them into the
botanical gardens.

"Look!" cried Laurel, pointing.
"They DO have rides."

Everyone looked where Laurel

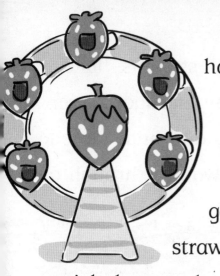

had pointed. There were rides shaped like vegetables and fruits: spinning garlic bulbs, flying strawberries, twirling artichokes, and a giant mushroom with lots of swings hanging from the mushroom cap.

"Rides at the end!" the guide said as she led the children deeper into the park.

They strolled by streams, lakes, and waterfalls. They zigzagged over a Japanese bridge and into a tea garden. Then they walked through a

topiary garden. "Topiary" meant that the trees and plants were trimmed into special shapes. Some trees were spiral shaped, and other trees looked like tutus stacked one on top of the other. Heidi liked the animal-shaped trees the best. She also really liked the unicorn and the stegosaurus.

"Incredible," whispered Heidi.

"Magical," Lucy whispered back.

The children learned about plants and flowers. They roamed through the Flitter Flutter butterfly meadow. When they got to the hedge maze,

Heidi heard a rumble in the distance. She looked at the sky. Dark gray clouds had rolled in. *That's strange,* she thought. *Is my wish running out?*

"Come on, Heidi!" said Lucy. "Let's get lost in the maze!"

The whole class disappeared into the hedges. Squeals and giggles filled

the paths as they raced around, but Heidi puttered along slowly. A gust of wind swirled through her hair as a raindrop plinked on her nose. *This is SO strange,* she said to herself. Then it thundered again— only this time a lot closer.

The guide blew a sharp whistle. "Everyone out of the maze!" she called.

Then all at once it began to pour.

# TOLD YOU SO

Lightning flashed across the clouds. Then *KABOOM!* Thunder exploded all around them. The children shrieked and scrambled out of the maze. Poor Lucy slipped and fell in the mud. Bruce leaned over to help her up, and his glasses fell on the ground. Before

he could pick them up, Melanie Maplethorpe ran by screaming and stepped on Bruce's glasses. The glasses snapped in half

Heidi stuffed her butterfly notebook under her shirt and hurried back the way she had come. The guide rounded everyone up. They huddled at the entrance to the maze. Soon golf carts lined up and carried them back to the bus in the parking garage.

"I am totally SOAKED!" complained
Melanie.

Lucy rolled her eyes. "We ALL are!"
she said.

"But I have on NICE clothes!"
Melanie wailed.

"Not anymore," said Bruce, who was pretty mad about his broken glasses.

It poured all the way back to school. The class didn't get to have a picnic in the fairy garden *or* have ice cream. And worst of all, they didn't get to go on the rides. Heidi hung her head. *This is all MY fault,* she thought. *My sunshine spell BACKFIRED. But how?* Heidi couldn't understand what had gone wrong. She sighed. *Let's face it,* she said to herself glumly. *I'm the WORST witch EVER.*

She didn't talk to anyone for the rest of the afternoon.

Heidi walked home from the bus stop in the rain. She dropped her backpack on the

mudroom floor. Then she slapped her soaked butterfly notebook onto the counter. Henry, who was sitting at the kitchen table, jumped out of his seat and stared at his sopping-wet sister.

"What happened to YOU?" Henry asked.

Heidi growled and opened the cup-
board to get a snack. Henry noticed
the notebook on the counter.

"Why is your notebook all soggy
and crumpled?" he questioned.

Heidi shut the cup-
board and glared at
her brother. "It got
rained on, *OKAY*?"
she said.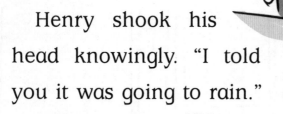

Henry shook his
head knowingly. "I told
you it was going to rain."

Heidi groaned dramatically. "Why

don't you just be
QUIET!" she yelled.
She stormed out of
the kitchen and then
ran to her bedroom.
Then Heidi thunked

into her desk chair.

"Merg!" Heidi was angry. She grabbed a fistful of wet hair and squeezed all the excess water out of it. A drop of water plinked into her straw  hat—the hat with the potion in it. Heidi sighed.

"Sometimes I wish I wasn't a witch!" she said.

Then she got up, shuffled to the bathroom, and turned on the shower to wash away this horrible day.

# Chapter 6

# A NEW RIDE

Mr. Doodlebee, the art teacher, handed out Styrofoam balls on a stick. He also handed out tissue paper, blocks of floral foam, and mini clay flowerpots.

"Today we're going to make topiary trees—just like the ones you saw on the field trip," he said. "Let's begin

by placing your floral foam in the
bottom of your flowerpot."

Heidi squished the foam into the
bottom of her pot.

"Then you carefully plant your
Styrofoam ball tree into the floral
foam."

Everybody pushed the sticks into the foam.

"Now crumple pieces of tissue paper and pin them onto the Styrofoam ball," he explained as he showed them how to do it. "You can make green leaves or any color you like."

Heidi crumpled a pile of green and lavender tissue paper. Then she decorated her topiary tree. She still felt awful about the field trip.

"Hey, Lucy, did you get the mud out of your clothes?" Heidi asked.

Lucy shook her head. "My mom tried everything."

Heidi sighed heavily. "I'm so sorry," she said.

Lucy tilted her head to one side. "It's not YOUR fault, Heidi."

Heidi bit her lip. "Oh, yes, it is," she muttered under her breath. "It's entirely my fault."

Then she turned to Bruce. "Will you be able to fix your glasses?" she asked.

Bruce squinted at Heidi. "Probably not," he said.

"Ugh," Heidi moaned. "That's too bad."

Then Melanie stood and cleared her throat, as if asking the whole class to look her way. "Well, I have GOOD news!" she said loudly.

"What is it?" asked Melanie's one and only best friend, Stanley Stonewrecker.

Melanie waited for everyone to pay attention. "Yesterday, I, Melanie Maplethorpe, got a brand-new BIKE."

"I'll bet it's pink," said Lucy. Everything Melanie got was pink.

"Of course it's pink!" Melanie smiled proudly. "And it's a beach cruiser with a straw basket and a  shiny silver bell on the handlebar."

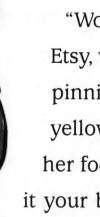

"Wow," said Eve Etsy, who was busy pinning a clump of yellow tissue onto her foam ball. "Was it your birthday?"

Melanie shook her head. "Nope."

"Then why did you get it?" asked Bruce.

"No reason," said Melanie as she sat back and admired her pink topiary. "Just because."

Heidi felt her face get hot. "How can you brag at a time like this?" she said angrily.

Melanie scowled. "What's wrong with YOU?" she said.

Heidi didn't usually have the courage to stand up to Melanie, but today she was too upset to care.

"Well, for your information, there are people in this room who lost IMPORTANT things in the rainstorm yesterday. And I doubt they want to hear about your new bike."

Melanie sniffed. "Well, for YOUR information, I was just trying to cheer them up," she said.

Then Mr. Doodlebee stepped in. "That's enough, girls!" he said firmly.

Heidi and Melanie looked down at their work.

Heidi had to hold back her tears. *I feel so crummy right now,* she thought.

# Chapter 7

# WITCH TO WITCH

Heidi knocked on Aunt Trudy's door after school. She always talked to her aunt about witch problems—that's because Aunt Trudy was a witch too, and so was Heidi's mother. But her mother never talked about witch stuff. She liked to be as normal as possible.

"Come in!" sang Aunt Trudy. Heidi walked into the living room and plunked onto the couch. A teakettle whistled in the kitchen.

"Are you hungry?" asked her aunt.

"Always," said Heidi.

Aunt Trudy went into the kitchen to get tea and snacks. Her two cats, Agnes and Hilda, jumped on the couch beside Heidi and began to cuddle with her.

Heidi heard the kettle stop whistling. China clinked as her aunt placed cups and plates on a tray.

Aunt Trudy returned and set the tray on the coffee table. Then she sat in a stuffed chair beside Heidi. Heidi helped herself to a slice of lemon cake with lemon icing.

"So," said her aunt as she sipped tea from a pink and green checkerboard cup, "what's on your mind?"

Heidi put the plate with lemon cake in her lap. "Basically, I'm a bad witch," she said, and took a bite of cake.

"Oh my," Aunt Trudy frowned. "Tell me what happened this time."

Heidi stared at her cake. "I cast a spell for an Everyday Wish and it backfired."

Aunt Trudy nodded. "And what did you wish for?" she questioned.

"I wished for sunny skies on our field trip," Heidi explained. "And it POURED."

"Oh dear," said Aunt Trudy.

"It gets worse," Heidi went on. "Lucy fell in the mud and ruined her best outfit, and Melanie stepped on Bruce's glasses"—she shook her head sadly—"and it was all my fault."

Aunt Trudy leaned back in her chair. "You may not want to hear

this," she began, "but this is *exactly* why your mother doesn't like you to use your witching skills at school."

Heidi sighed. "I know. It ALWAYS gets me in trouble."

Aunt Trudy nodded and sipped her tea. "But maybe you will feel better if you do something nice for your friends."

Heidi's face brightened. "Hey! That

WOULD make me feel better," she said. "But what?"

"Well, you could offer to help clean Lucy's outfit," suggested her aunt.

"And maybe fix Bruce's glasses!" Heidi chimed in.

She clanked her plate on the table. The cats leaped to the floor.

"I've got to get going!" she said as she realized she might be able to fix the mess she had made. Then she kissed her aunt on the cheek and sailed out the door.

Aunt Trudy chuckled and shook her head.

# A LOSS FOR WORDS

Heidi picked a daisy still damp with dew on the way into the house. Then she measured two teaspoons of powdered sugar, plucked three more lemon gumdrops from the side of the old gingerbread house, and zoomed to her room. She gently shut the door

behind her. Then she emptied the old potion into the wastebasket and added the fresh ingredients.

Heidi read the directions extra carefully. This time she noticed that the spell came with a warning.

*Remember to be careful what you wish for.*

*Perfect,* she said to herself. *Because these wishes are important!*

She slipped on her Witches of Westwick medallion and stirred the ingredients. Then, with one hand on her medallion and the other over the hat, she chanted the spell.

*"I wish I may, I wish I might, wish this wish so big and bright."*

Heidi squeezed her eyes shut and made her first wish. "I wish Lucy's outfit would be sparkling clean!"

She waited a moment for the magic to work. Then she chanted the spell again and made her second wish. "I wish Bruce's glasses would be as good as new!"

After that, Heidi ran to the phone. She called Lucy first. Mrs. Lancaster

74

put Lucy on the line.

"Hi, Lucy," Heidi said. "How are your muddy clothes?"

"They're out on the clothesline. My mom put lemon juice on the mud stains and hung them in the sun."

"I bet they are clean now. Can you please go check?" Heidi urged.

"Okay. Be right back," said Lucy, setting down the phone.

Heidi smiled to herself. *Boy, is Lucy going to be surprised when she finds her outfit is as good as new!* She heard Lucy pick up the phone.

"So, are they back to normal?" blurted Heidi excitedly.

"No, still stained," Lucy said.

Heidi stared at the phone in disbelief.

"Are you still there, Heidi?" Lucy asked.

"Yup, I'm still here," said Heidi glumly. "I'm sorry about your outfit."

"Me too," said Lucy.

"But thanks for calling."

Heidi called Bruce next. He pulled out his glasses from the wastebasket. "Still broken," he said.

Heidi got off the phone and walked slowly back to her room. *Is it me?* she wondered. *Or is it the spell that's not working?* Heidi picked up her *Book of Spells* to see where she had gone wrong this time.

Then she noticed something very strange. As she reread the spell, the words began to *disappear* from the page. Heidi blinked and looked again. The words continued to vanish, one by one, right before her eyes! Heidi gasped.

"What's happening?" she cried.

Soon the whole book was blank.

Heidi snapped the book shut.

*This is SERIOUS!* she said to herself.

*I need to get to Aunt Trudy right away!*

## Chapter 9

# OOPS-A-DAISY!

Heidi dashed to Aunt Trudy's and pounded on the door until her aunt opened it. "Good heavens, Heidi! What's the matter?" she asked.

Heidi threw her arms around her aunt and began to cry.

"Hush, hush, dear," Aunt Trudy said

gently. "Everything's going to be all right." She walked Heidi inside, and they sat on the couch together. Aunt Trudy offered Heidi a tissue. Heidi plucked one from the box.

"Something awful is happening to me," she wailed. "And I don't know what it is!"

"Talk to me," Aunt Trudy said.

Heidi dabbed her eyes with the tissue. "It all started when my wishing spell didn't work," she said, sniffling. "I tried to fix everything with other wishing spells, but those didn't work

either. And THEN, when I checked the *Book of Spells* to see where I went wrong, the words on the page DISAPPEARED."

Aunt Trudy tapped her finger on her cheek thoughtfully.

"Hmm," she said. "We need to retrace exactly what you did."

Heidi nodded.

"Now, did you make any sub-stitutions in your spell?" her aunt questioned.

Heidi thought for a moment.

"Well, I did make my own flower dew," she remembered. "Yes, I used a daisy from Mom's garden and sprinkled it with tap water."

Aunt Trudy raised her eyebrows. "Oops-a-daisy," she said. "That's a problem. You can substitute rain-water for dew, but *not* tap water."

"Oh, so THAT'S why my wish for sunny skies didn't work," said Heidi. "But it still doesn't explain why I've lost my powers."

Aunt Trudy crossed her arms and looked deep in thought.

"Hmm. Everyday Wish spells have a warning, don't they?" asked her aunt. "It's in the fine print under the spell."

Heidi nodded. "Yes. It says to be careful what you wish for. And I was!"

"You're probably right," said her aunt. "But let's review everything you did that day to see if we can find more clues."

So Heidi told Aunt Trudy everything: She told her about the trip to the botanical gardens and her bad mood at school. She told her about getting soaked on the way home from the bus stop. She even mentioned her argument with Henry. "Then I went to my room, wrung the rainwater out of my hair, and jumped in the shower."

Aunt Trudy sat thoughtfully as she listened to Heidi review the day.

"Were you anywhere near your potion when you wrung out your hair?" she asked.

Heidi thought for a moment.

"I was sitting at my desk," she remembered. "The straw hat with the potion was on my desk in front of me."

Aunt Trudy smiled. "Aha! Now we're getting somewhere," she said. "Think back. Did you make any wishes while you were at your desk?"

Heidi shook her head. "I don't think so," she said.

But then her eyes grew wide. "Wait a minute—I DID!" she recalled. "I wished . . . I wished I wasn't a witch anymore! Oh no!"

Aunt Trudy held her arms out wide. "And there you have it!" she said triumphantly.

Heidi's face fell. "But how can I undo my wish?" she asked sadly.

Aunt Trudy patted Heidi's leg. "There's only one way to reverse a wish like that," she said.

Heidi looked at her aunt hopefully.

"You must find three people who make a wish in your presence," Aunt Trudy explained. "Then you have to grant each wish without magic."

"WITHOUT magic?" Heidi said in disbelief.

"Oh yes, without magic," her aunt repeated.

Heidi flopped against the back of the couch. "More like oh no," she moaned. "Without magic this is going to be IMPOSSIBLE!"

# Chapter 10

# WISHY-WASHY

*B-r-r-r-r-ing!*

The bell rang for recess. Heidi shoved her math book into her desk. She had decided she would do whatever it took to get her powers back. And now was her chance. She bounded down the stairs to the playground and caught up to Lucy and Bruce.

"Got any wishes?" she asked, using the straightforward approach.

Lucy and Bruce wrinkled their brows.

"I mean, if you could wish for anything in the world, what would it be?" asked Heidi.

"Um, I've got one," Lucy began. "I guess I've always wished I could have my own panda bear."

Heidi frowned. "That's unrealistic," she said.

"I know," said Lucy, "but it's something I've always wished for."

Bruce pushed his new glasses up the bridge of his nose. "Well, I wish I had a supercomputer," he said.

Heidi tipped her head to one side. "Not sure I can help you with that one, either," she said.

Bruce laughed. "I wasn't expecting you to!" he said.

Heidi turned to Laurel. "Do you have a wish?"

Laurel scratched her head. "I wish I had a slide that went from my bedroom all the way down into my very own swimming pool."

Heidi jerked her head back. "You're kidding—right?"

Laurel shook her head. "Why would I ever joke about a thing like that?" she said.

Then Melanie, who was listening in as usual, tapped Heidi on the shoulder. "You know what I'd wish for?" she said.

Heidi could only imagine.

"I'd wish for a brand-new beach cruiser bicycle, but since I already GOT that, I'd wish for a pet unicorn," she said.

Heidi rolled her eyes. "Oh, brother," she said. "This is going to be harder than I thought."

Melanie scowled. "And what's that supposed to mean?" she said.

Heidi looked at Melanie's puzzled face. "Oh, never mind," she said. "You wouldn't understand." Then Heidi turned up her nose and walked away, which was usually what Melanie did. But today it was Heidi's turn.

# Chapter 11

# GOING THROUGH HOOPS

Heidi leaped over the hopscotch course without one single hop. *How am I supposed to grant wishes without magic?* she wondered to herself. Then she heard someone shout something from the basketball court. She looked over. A basketball had gotten stuck between the hoop and the backboard.

"I wish we could get our ball down!" shouted a fourth-grade girl named Carly Coleman. Carly banged on the basketball post with the palm of her hand.

Heidi stopped in her tracks. *A WISH!* she said to herself.

She scanned the playground for something that would reach the basketball hoop. There was a broom

leaning against the side of the school building near the court. It belonged to Mr. Fortini, the janitor. He was rak-ing leaves far off by the swings.

*He won't miss his broom for a minute,* Heidi thought. She sprinted across the blacktop and grabbed the broom.

Then she raced back to the basketball hoop.

"I can help!" Heidi said. She jabbed at the ball with the broom. It came free and fell to the ground. *Hmm . . . maybe a witch really can do magic with a broom,* she thought.

Carly grabbed the ball. "Thanks!" she said.

"Anytime," Heidi said, and then she returned the broom to where she had found it. Mr. Fortini waved at Heidi. She waved back.

*One wish down, two to go,* Heidi said to herself. She looked at the clock on top of the school building. There was only fifteen minutes of recess left. She would have to work fast.

# Chapter 12

# NO PROBLEM!

Heidi scouted the playground for more kids with wishes. She visited the swings and saw Henry trying to pump his legs. He hadn't quite learned how to swing.

"Will you give me a push?" he asked when he saw his sister.

Heidi grabbed Henry's swing from
behind and gave him a push.

"Wheeee!" Henry cried. "Again!"

"Only if you say 'I WISH you'd push
me again!'" said Heidi. But Henry
didn't like being told what to do.

"Again!" he cried.

"Push me, too!" shouted Dudley, Henry's best friend, who sat on the swing beside him.

Heidi moved to Dudley's swing and pushed him as hard as she could.

"Again!" shouted Henry and Dudley.

"Not now," said Heidi. "I'm on a wishing mission." She walked away

and strolled around the monkey bars and the slide, but she didn't find any wishers. Then Heidi noticed Stanley Stonewrecker sitting on a bench with his math book open. She wandered over and sat down beside him.

"What's up?" Heidi asked.

Stanley let out a big sigh. "I'm working on math homework," he said. "I wish someone could explain how to solve word problems. I stink at them."

Heidi scooched closer to Stanley.

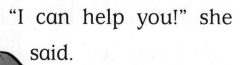

"I can help you!" she said.

Stanley was surprised and looked up at Heidi. "Really? You'd do that?"

"Definitely!" said Heidi. "Give me a problem."

Stanley pointed to the word problem he'd been working on and read it out loud. "'Mia's mom baked forty-one cookies. Scott's dad baked thirty-eight cookies. Mia sampled three cookies. Scott sampled four cookies. How many cookies made it to the school party?'"

Heidi studied the problem. "This is easy," she said.

"Not for me," said Stanley. "Word problems get me all mixed up."

"If you write down each step, it's easier," Heidi said. "Let's see your notebook."

Stanley handed Heidi his math notebook and pencil.

Heidi read the problem again.

"First we have to add up how many

cookies there are altogether," she said. She wrote out the equation.

$$41 + 38 =$$

Stanley looked at the problem.

"I can solve that!" he said. He added the numbers together. Heidi did the same.

"I got seventy-nine," Stanley said.

"Me too," said Heidi. "Okay, now let's subtract how many cookies Mia ate." Heidi wrote down the next equation.

79 - 3 =

Stanley subtracted the numbers on his fingers.

"Um . . . seventy-six!" he cried.

Heidi nodded. "Now we need to subtract the cookies Scott ate," she said. She wrote down the next step.

76 - 4 =

Stanley subtracted the numbers. "Seventy-two!" he said happily.

"That's right!" said Heidi. "And seventy-two is the answer."

Mrs. Welli blew her whistle. Heidi's classmates started running toward the school building.

"Thanks, Heidi," said Stanley as he closed his math book. "You really helped me."

"No problem!" Heidi replied. Then she laughed. "Get it? No PROBLEM, as in WORD problem?"

Stanley laughed.

They headed back to school with the rest of their class.

*Another wish down!* Heidi said to herself. *One more to go!*

# Chapter 13

# A GOOD HELPER

Heidi listened for wishes all day, but nobody wished for anything. *Maybe I can MAKE people wish for something,* she thought. Heidi got started right away. First she bumped into Lucy's desk on purpose. *Clunk!* Lucy's pencil case fell onto the floor.

"I'm SO sorry!" Heidi said dramatically. She waited for Lucy to wish for Heidi to pick it up. But Lucy didn't wish, she just asked.

"Um, Heidi, would you please pick that up?" she said.

Heidi grabbed the pencil case and plopped it onto Lucy's desk.

*Oh well, so much for that one*, she thought.

Then it was time for drama class.

Heidi passed out scripts for *Jack and the Beanstalk*.

"Is there anything else I can help you with, Mrs. Noddywonks?" asked Heidi.

Mrs. Noddywonks looked down over the top of her reading glasses and smiled.

"How thoughtful of you to ask, Heidi," said the drama teacher. "Would you please arrange the chairs in a circle for acting warm-ups?"

Heidi nodded and headed for the stack of folding chairs. *Merg,* she thought. *Why didn't she WISH for me to set up the chairs?* But Heidi mindfully unfolded the chairs and set them in a circle.

Then everyone sat down to play Jumping Jelly Beans. Mrs. Noddywonks called out types of beans, and the children acted them out.

"French bean!" Mrs. Noddywonks called.

Everyone raised their hands to their chins. "Ooh la la!" they cried.

Then it was time for library.

"Mrs. Williams, do you need any help?" Heidi asked the school librarian.

"As a matter of fact, I do!" Mrs. Williams handed Heidi a pair of rubber gloves and a tall stack of white coffee filters. Then she pointed to a tub of blue dye sitting on a table covered in newspaper.

"Please soak the coffee filters in the dye and set them out to dry," said

Mrs. Williams. "These will become the water for our Under-the-Sea Book Fair decorations."

Heidi stretched on the rubber gloves and soaked the coffee filters in the dye. *This is fun,* she thought, *even though Mrs. Williams didn't wish for my help.*

In gym, Heidi saw stray basketballs all over the gym floor. She walked up to Coach Wardner.

"Don't you WISH someone would pick up all those basketballs?" Heidi asked.

Coach Wardner chuckled a bit and shook his head. "Not really, since we're about to play basketball," he said. "But you're welcome to pick them up *after* class."

So Heidi helped collect the basket-balls after class.

"That shows great sportsmanship, Heidi!" Coach Wardner said, praising her. He held up his fist, and Heidi bumped it.

*Well, I may not have my powers back,* Heidi thought, *but it sure has been fun to help everyone out.*

# Chapter 14

# PEDAL PUSHER

"I'm going scootering!" shouted Heidi when she got home from school.

"Stay on the sidewalk!" Mom called from her office.

"Okay!" said Heidi as the door leading to the garage slammed behind her.

Heidi unhooked her scooter, put on her purple helmet, and then took off down the driveway and onto the empty sidewalk. She cruised along, kicking off with her right foot. She rolled over cracks. *Click-clack! Click-clack!* Up ahead she saw a girl trying to ride a bike. The girl wobbled unsteadily and then tipped over and fell into a very large bush.

*Uh-oh!* thought Heidi. *I'd better go help!*

Heidi whizzed down the sidewalk. As she got closer, she realized the girl was Melanie Maplethorpe! Heidi wanted to turn around and go home.

But how could she? Melanie was cry-
ing. Heidi rolled up to Melanie and
stopped.

"Are you okay?" Heidi asked.

Melanie shook her head. "I'm stuck
in my pedals," she said, sniffling.

Heidi lay down her scooter. Then she untangled the bike from Melanie's feet. Melanie got up. She had a scrape on her knee.

"Does it sting?" Heidi asked.

Melanie nodded.

"Hey, don't worry," said Heidi. "It'll be okay."

Melanie wiped her tears away with her hands.

"Would you like me to ride home with you?" asked Heidi. Melanie lived on the same street as Heidi.

Melanie shook her head and started to cry again.

"Oh no. What's the matter now?" Heidi asked.

Melanie sniffed. "Just go away!" she said.

Instead, Heidi folded her arms and tapped her foot. "Why can't you just let me help?" she said.

Melanie rubbed her eyes. "Okay, FINE!" she said. "The truth is, I don't know how to ride my new bike and I wish I did!"

Heidi stopped tapping her foot. "You WISH you did?" she repeated as she felt a smile spread over her face. "I can grant you your wish!"

Melanie threw Heidi a funny look. "What are you, some sort of magic genie in a bottle?" she questioned.

"Me? Of course not," squeaked Heidi nervously. "But I CAN show you

how to ride a bike."

Heidi leaned over and picked up the pink bike.

"Here's what you do," said Heidi. She rolled the bike to a slope in the side-walk. "First you roll without using the pedals. Watch."

Heidi sat on the bike and pushed her feet on the ground. She rolled down the sidewalk.

Then she rode the bike back to Melanie. "Here, you try."

Melanie got on the bike and slowly let the bike roll down the slope. The handlebars wiggled uncertainly as she tried to get her balance. Then she

got off the bike and walked it back up the slope. She tried it again and again until she didn't wobble anymore.

"This time use the pedals," Heidi suggested.

Melanie pedaled slowly at first, but soon she got the hang of it.

"Wow, Melanie, you learned really fast," cheered Heidi.

"Thanks," said Melanie. "That was nice of you to help me."

"No problem," said Heidi. "Maybe we can go for a bike ride sometime." Heidi could hardly believe she let those words come out of her mouth.

"No way, Heidi Heckelbeck," said Melanie, but she had a slight smile on her face.

Heidi picked up her scooter. "See you around," she said.

"See ya," said Melanie.

Heidi rolled down the sidewalk. She felt a warm glow come over her body. She smiled. *My powers must be back!* she said to herself. *I can feel it.*

She raced home and darted up the stairs to her room. Then Heidi reached under the bed and pulled out her *Book of Spells*.

"Oh please, oh please, oh please work," Heidi said as she opened the book.

All the inside pages were still blank. But then the words slowly reappeared with a bright green glow on each page! It had worked! Even the cover of her *Book of Spells* had changed! It used to be black, but now it was purple with the sweetest swirls all over! Heidi hugged her new book so tightly. "I'm never, ever, ever going to lose you again. And that's a promise!"

Then she jumped back on her scooter and zipped over to Aunt Trudy's. She couldn't wait to tell her the good news.

Check out the next book starring

HEIDI HECKELBECK

*Flit!*

*Fly!*

*Flutter!*

Fall leaves swirled and ticked the panes of Heidi's window. She pulled the hem of her quilt up to her chin. *I love fall!* she said to herself happily. Then she remembered something else she loved: sweater weather! And

An excerpt from *Heidi Heckelbeck and the Big Mix Up*

the best part was, Heidi had a brand-new sweater.

She hopped out of bed and slipped on her fuzzy bunny slippers. Then she shuffled to her dresser and opened the bottom drawer. There it was—her new light gray sweater. It had pink buttons up the front and pink stripes down the sleeves. On the lower right-hand side was an embroidered brown mouse sitting in a white teacup. Heidi had gotten the sweater at Miss Harriet's store.

*And now I finally get to wear it!* she thought. She pulled on a jean skirt and a yellow tank top. Then she snuggled into her new sweater. She posed this way and that in front of the mirror. "Oh, it's SO cute!" she declared. Then she skipped downstairs to breakfast.

"Mmm," she murmured as she stepped into the kitchen. "What smells so good?"

Henry tapped the side of his head with his finger. "Hmm, let me think," he said. "Probably not YOU!"

Heidi rolled her eyes.

Heidi frowned at her brother. "Way to go, little bro," she said.

An excerpt from *Heidi Heckelbeck and the Big Mix Up*

Henry shrugged. "Sometimes my clothes get hungry," he said. "Maybe that little mousie on your sweater wants some oatmeal too!"

"Not if I can help it," Heidi said as she placed a napkin in her lap.

Mom gave her a wink and a smile. "By the way, Heidi, I heard from Mrs. Welli that you have a publishing party at school on Friday. Parents are invited to hear students read their stories."

"Sounds like fun!" said Dad as he joined the family at the table. "Do you know what you're going to write?"

Heidi blew on a spoonful of oatmeal. "Not yet," she said. "But I want it to be something special."

Then she took a big bite and gave her dad a thumbs-up. "I wonder if it would it be too mushy to write about this oatmeal . . . because it's super-yummers!"

An excerpt from *Heidi Heckelbeck and the Big Mix Up*